Summer

Flowers bloom
in the warm,
sunny days
of summer.

purple
delphinium

sweet
honeysuckle

fluttering
butterflies

Autumn

Many leaves
change colour
in the autumn.

Leaves
fall...

...berries
ripen...

...and fruits
are ready
to eat.

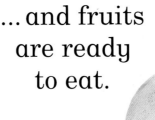

Winter

Only a few plants can grow in the cold winter earth.

winter pansy

prickly holly

trailing ivy

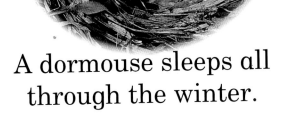

A dormouse sleeps all through the winter.

Weather

Which weather do you like the best?

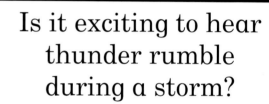

Is it exciting to hear thunder rumble during a storm?

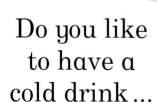

Do you like to have a cold drink ...

... on a hot, sunny day?

When there is crisp
snow on the ground...

...do you like
to play with
snowballs?

What kind
of weather
do you need
to fly a kite?

In the garden

Flowers, birds, trees and insects live in gardens.

Do you like gardening?

fierce, stripey wasps

tall tulip

slender gladioli

purple iris

frilly carnation

slithery
snails

shiny blackbird

spotty
ladybird

Which kind of
flowers do
you like best?

scented
freesia

thorny
rose

In the forest

Animals, birds
and insects live
amongst the
tall trees.

noisy
woodpecker

nimble
squirrel

prickly
pine cone

feathery ferns

What can you see in this forest?

sleek fox

shy rabbit

On the beach

Shells and seaweed
are washed up
on to the beach.

sandy
sea lion

noisy seagull

Have you ever seen a
crab scuttling sideways?

slippery
seaweed

tropical sandy beach

Some sea
creatures live
in shells.

Do you like
building
castles in
the sand?

Under the sea

Lots of amazing
plants and
creatures live
under the sea.

dangerous shark

spotty lobster

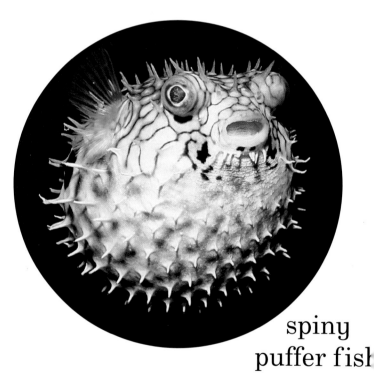

spiny
puffer fish

brittle, feathery coral

Have you ever tried snorkelling in the sea?

brightly striped tropical fish

Ponds

Lots of different plants and animals like to live in, or near, water.

waterlilies

lush, green pond

blotchy, brown frog

A shimmering stickleback swims about under the water.

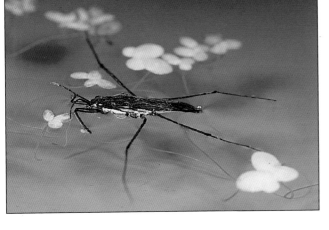

gliding pond skater

Can you waddle like a duck?

darting dragonfly

Minibeasts

Minibeasts creep, crawl and scuttle everywhere.

creepy-crawly woodlice

wiggly worm

marching ants

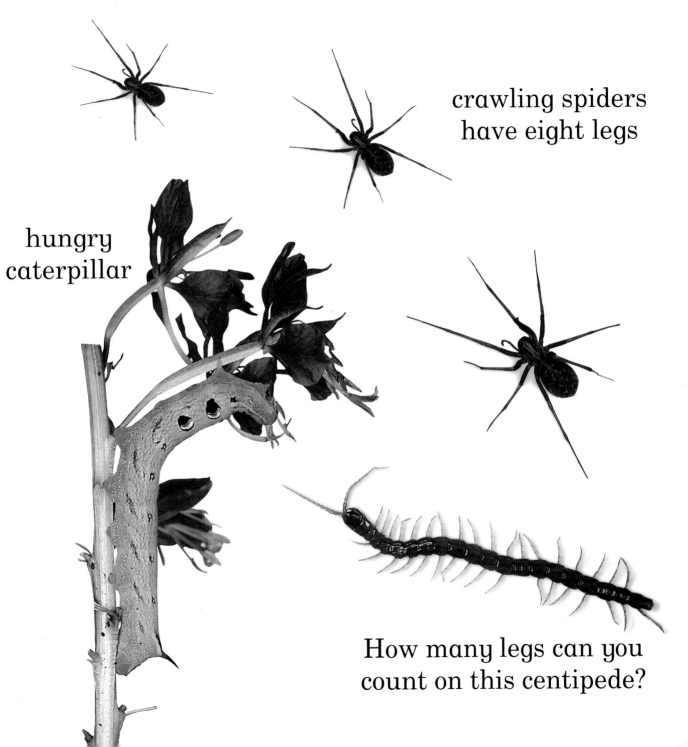

crawling spiders
have eight legs

hungry
caterpillar

How many legs can you
count on this centipede?

Can you remember where these things are found?

let's
ook at
nature

Nicola Tuxworth

Spring

Spring is the season when everything starts to grow.

Fluffy chicks are born...

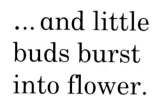

...trees uncurl their leaves...

...and little buds burst into flower.